DATE DUE

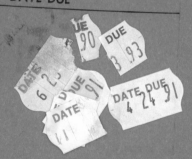

James Stevenson

Emma at the Beach

Greenwillow Books, New York

Printed in Hong Kong
by South China Printing
Company (1988) Ltd.

First Edition
10 9 8 7 6 5 4 3 2 1

Library of Congress
Cataloging-in-Publication Data

Stevenson, James (date)
Emma at the beach /
James Stevenson.
p.   cm.
Summary:
Mean witches Dolores
and Lavinia torment
Emma and her
friends and retreat
to the cool comfort
of the beach,
but their victims
strike back with
a creative form
of revenge.
ISBN 0-688-08806-6.
ISBN 0-688-08807-4 (lib. bdg.)
[1. Witches—Fiction.
2. Beaches—Fiction.
3. Cartoons and comics.]
I. Title.
PZ7.S84748Eo 1990
[E]—dc19
88-34918   CIP   AC